We Love Underpants!

Three Pants-tastic Books in One

Claire Freedman & Ben Cort

SIMON & SCHUSTER

London New York Sydney Toronto New Delhi

For Jason, my forever friend
~ CF

For Ruth, Johnny and Anna, with all my love
~ BC

Aliens Love
Underpants

Aliens love underpants,
Of every shape and size.
But there are no underpants in space,
So here's a big surprise . . .

When aliens fly down to Earth,
They don't come to meet YOU . . . .
They simply want your underpants –
I'll bet you never knew!

Their spaceship's radar bleeps and blinks
The moment that it sees
A washing line of underpants,
All flapping in the breeze.

They land in your back garden,
Though they haven't been invited.
"Oooooh, UNDERPANTS!" they chant,
And dance around, delighted.

They like them red, they like them green,
Or orange like satsumas.
But best of all they love the sight,
Of Granny's spotted bloomers.

Mum's pink frilly knickers
Are a perfect place to hide
And Grandpa's woolly long johns
Make a super-whizzy slide.

In daring competitions,
Held up by just one peg,
They count how many aliens
Can squeeze inside each leg.

They wear pants on their feet and heads
And other silly places.
They fly pants from their spaceships and
Hold Upside-Down-Pant Races!

As they go zinging through the air,
It really is pants–tastic.
What fun the aliens can have,
With pingy pants elastic!

It's not your neighbour's naughty dog,
Or next-door's funny game.
When underpants go missing,
The ALIENS are to blame!

But quick! Mum's coming out to fetch
The washing in at last.
Wheee! Off the aliens all zoom,
They're used to leaving fast . . .

So when you put your pants on,
Freshly washed and nice and clean,
Just check in case an alien
Still lurks inside, unseen!

To Dr. M.J. Smith
~ CF

♥

For Doreen and family, with love
~ BC

♥

Monsters Love
Underpants

Monsters think it's MONSTER fun,
To creep around, all scary!
But there's something they love even MORE,
Than looking mean and hairy!

Monsters all LOVE underpants,
And think pants are fun-tastic.
They like all patterns, shapes and styles,
And twanging pants elastic!

Some prowl through dingy dungeons, "Oooooow!"
You hear them howling, loudly.
CREAK! One finds squeaky armour pants,
And clanks around SO proudly!

Drool monsters from the steamy swamp,
Fill pants with gooey slime.
But, OOOOPS! Their pants get slippery,
And slide down all the time!

Wild, woolly mountain monsters
Make explorers faint with fright!
CLOMP! They snatch their frozen pants,
Then run off in the night!

At the bottom of the ocean,
A pirate ship now rests,
Where sea monsters wear pants with jewels,
They've pinched from treasure chests!

The spiky, spooky, space monsters
All wave and roar, "Hooray!"
When out from blackest, deepest space,
Bright bloomers float their way!

It's not the sand inside his pants
That makes this monster tetchy.
His underpants are way too small,
"I wish they were more stretchy!"

It's Saturday - their Disco Night,
Held in a secret cave.
The password (sshh!) is WOBBLY PANTS!
To get inside the rave.

The monsters show their pants off,
As they dance The Monster Bop.
Their pants-clad bottoms jig and jive,
Till someone yells out "STOP!"

"It's almost daylight! Quick, back home . . .
We can't risk being spotted!
For no one will be scared of us,
In pants all striped and dotted!"

So if you hear strange scuffles
From beneath your bed – beware!
You might just catch a monster,
Trying on YOUR snazzy pair!

For Sheniz and Noah
~ CF
♥
For Nia
~ BC
♥

Aliens Love Dinopants

A band of pants-mad aliens
Zoomed down here, when SURPRISE!
Bright lightning hit their spaceship, BANG!
And hurled them from the skies.

Crash-landing in thick jungle,
"Whoops!" the aliens gasped. "Oh dear!"
But their pants-tracker was BLEEPING.
How could underpants be here?

The aliens trekked through tangly trees,
The signal getting stronger.
Through slimy swamps, down deep ravines,
Could they go on much longer?

Their tracker went BLEEP BONKERS!
"Wow! We must be close," they cried.
It led them to a hidden gate.
"Let's take a peep inside!"

BLEEP! BLEEP! YIPPEE!
They'd found them
(Those aliens are so clever!)
A stash of such gigantic pants,
Each pair could stretch forever!

"We'll take these pants!" the aliens laughed.
But . . . RAAAAR! They heard loud roars!
And found themselves surrounded BY . . .

GINORMOUS DINOSAURS!

The dinosaurs were furious.
"Hands off our pants!" they roared.
"We'll fight you pesky aliens,
To save our precious hoard!"

The aliens almost fainted!

"DINOSAURS? This can't be so!

You dinos were wiped out from Earth,

Pants-zillion years ago!"

"We hid down here," the dinos said.
"The humans didn't see!
We saved our pants, but daren't come out.
We wish we could roam free!"

"We ALL love pants," one alien cheered,
"So there's no need to fight!
I have a plan to get you out
And save you from your plight!"

Those busy aliens got to work,
With laser tools and saws.
They hammered, welded, chopped and drilled,
Helped by the dinosaurs.

"TA-DAH! A super dino-pod
To launch you into space!
We'll take you to our planet,
ZOOM! A most pants-tastic place!"

"Our new home's great!" the dinos said.
"There's underpants for all!"
It's fun the games that can be played
With pants both HUGE and small.

So when your washing's on the line,
Quick! Guard it at the double.
With aliens AND dinosaurs,
There's twice pants-pinching trouble!

Look out for more
pants-tastic adventures
from Claire Freedman
and Ben Cort!

Aliens in Underpants Save the World
Claire Freedman & Ben Cort

Aliens Love Panta Claus
Claire Freedman & Ben Cort

Dinosaurs Love Underpants
Claire Freedman & Ben Cort

Pirates Love Underpants
Claire Freedman and Ben Cort

SIMON & SCHUSTER

This collection first published in Great Britain in 2021 by Simon & Schuster UK Ltd
1st Floor, 222 Gray's Inn Road, London, WC1X 8HB

Aliens Love Underpants published in 2007
Monsters Love Underpants published in 2014
Aliens Love Dinopants published in 2015

Text copyright © 2007, 2014, 2015 Claire Freedman • Illustrations copyright © 2007, 2014, 2015 Ben Cort

The right of Claire Freedman and Ben Cort to be identified as the author and illustrator of this work has been
asserted by them in accordance with the Copyright, Design and Patents Act, 1988

A CIP catalogue record for this book is available from the British Library

PB 978-1-3985-0012-9 • eBook 978-1-3985-0013-6

Printed in China

1 3 5 7 9 10 8 6 4 2

OLIVIA

...and the Missing Toy

7

8

9

10

11

12

To David with great love and thanks for almost everything

SIMON AND SCHUSTER
First published in Great Britain in 2003 by Simon & Schuster UK Ltd
1st Floor, 222 Gray's Inn Road, London WC1X 8HB

First published in 2003 by Atheneum Books for Young Readers,
an imprint of Simon & Schuster Children's Publishing Division, New York

This paperback edition first published in Great Britain in 2006

A CIP catalogue record for this book is available from the British Library upon request

Book design by Ann Bobco
The text for this book was set in Centaur
The illustrations are rendered in charcoal and gouache on paper

ISBN: 978 1 416 91744 1

Printed in Italy

3 5 7 9 10 8 6 4

Grateful acknowledgment to:
• The Griffith Institute, Oxford, for permission to use the photo on p. 7 of the Sphinx.
• Barbara Morgan Archives for permission to use the photo on p. 9 of Martha Graham, *Letter to the World*
(Kick), 1940, copyright © Barbara Morgan, Barbara Morgan Archives.

OLIVIA

...and the Missing Toy

by Ian Falconer

SIMON AND SCHUSTER

London   New York   Sydney

One day Olivia was riding a camel in Egypt . . .

when her mother woke her up. "Time to get up, sweetie-pie. Remember, you have soccer this morning."

Olivia's uniform comes in a really unattractive green.

"Mummy, can you make
me a red soccer shirt
like this one? Please? . . ."

"But then you'll look
different from everyone
else on the team,"
explained her mother.

"That's the point."

When Olivia came home
from practice, her mother
was working on the shirt.
"Is it done yet?" she asked.
"Not yet," said her mother.

Olivia waited,

and waited,

and waited,

till she was too exhausted to wait any longer.

So she went out to play with the cat.

"Look, darling, it's all done!" said her mother.

But something was missing.
"Wait a second," said Olivia.

"Where's
my
toy?"

"Where's my toy? It was right there on the bed. I just put it there. I remember exactly. That's my best toy. I need it now! Somebody took my best toy!"

Olivia looked everywhere –

under the rug,

under the sofa,

under the cat.

She asked her little brother, Ian,
"WHAT DID YOU DO WITH MY TOY?"

She asked her baby brother, William,

"WHAT DID YOU DO WITH MY TOY?"

"Wooshee gaga."

That night,
and it was a dark and stormy night,
Olivia was practising her piano
when she heard an awful sound.

The sound got louder
and louder.
It was
HORRIBLE,
and it was coming
from behind
the door.

So, of course, Olivia went inside.

And that's when
she saw it. It was . . .

"Mummy, Daddy, Mummy, Daddy! It was Perry!" cried Olivia.
"He took my best toy and chewed it to bits, and now it's wrecked."

"I'm sorry, sweetie-pie," said her mother, "but doggies like to chew.
And he didn't know it was your toy."

"My *best* toy."

"Don't worry," said Olivia's father.
"Tomorrow we'll go get you the *very* best toy in the whole world."

"Oh, thank you, Daddy. I love you more than anyone."

Still, it *was* Olivia's best toy. So she fixed it,

adding a bow for extra beauty.

All better.

"Only books about cats tonight, Mummy."

But even Olivia couldn't stay mad forever.

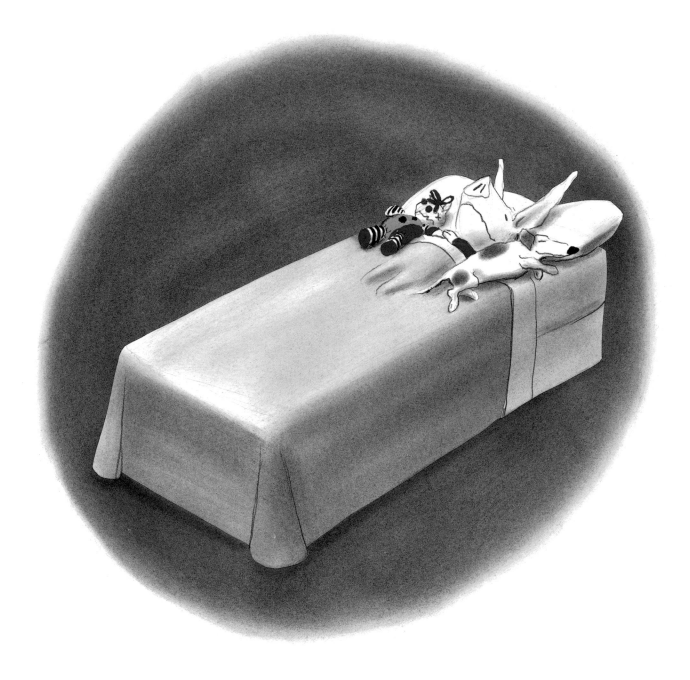

1

2

3

4

5

6

7

8

9

10

11

12